MASQUERADE MEOW

BEYOND THE ARISTOCRACY

LINDA RAE SANDE

Twisted Teacup
PUBLISHING

ALSO BY LINDA RAE SANDE

The Daughters of the Aristocracy

The Kiss of a Viscount

The Grace of a Duke

The Seduction of an Earl

The Sons of the Aristocracy

Tuesday Nights

The Widowed Countess

My Fair Groom

The Sisters of the Aristocracy

The Story of a Baron

The Passion of a Marquess

The Desire of a Lady

The Brothers of the Aristocracy

The Love of a Rake

The Caress of a Commander

The Epiphany of an Explorer

The Widows of the Aristocracy

The Gossip of an Earl

The Enigma of a Widow

The Secrets of a Viscount

The Widowers of the Aristocracy

The Dream of a Duchess

The Vision of a Viscountess

The Conundrum of a Clerk

The Charity of a Viscount

The Cousins of the Aristocracy

The Promise of a Gentleman

The Pride of a Gentleman

The Holidays of the Aristocracy

The Christmas of a Countess

The Knot of a Knight

The Holiday of a Marquess

The Winter Kiss of a Rogue

The Snow Angel of a Duke

The Ivy of an Earl

The Heirs of the Aristocracy

The Angel of an Astronomer

The Puzzle of a Bastard

The Choice of a Cavalier

The Bargain of a Baroness

The Jewel of an Earl's Heir

The Vixen of a Viscount

The Honor of an Heir

The Rose of a Sultan's Son

The Ladies of the Aristocracy

The Lady of a Grump

The Lady of a Sultan

The Pursuit of a Duchess

The Lords of the Aristocracy

The Abduction of an Earl

Beyond the Aristocracy

The Pleasure of a Pirate

The Making of a Mistress

The Bride of a Baronet

The Caton of a Captain

Puss and Pots

The Betrothal of a Baron

Masquerade Meow

The Grand Tours of the Aristocracy

A Courtship in Catania

An Affaire in Athens

A Lover in Luxor

A Rogue in Rome

Revenge of the Wallflowers

The Wager of a Wallflower

Stella of Akrotiri

Origins

Deminon

Diana

The Lyon's Den (Dragonblade Publishing)

The Courage of a Lyon

The Lady of a Lyon

The Loyalty of a Lyon

Note: Translations of select titles are available in German, Italian, Spanish and Portuguese.

CHAPTER 1
A CAT CONFOUNDS A CUSTOMER

ctober 1862, Montgomery Dry Goods and Mercantile, Galena, Illinois

Even before the faint tinkle of the door's bell signaled another arrival to Montgomery Dry Goods, Ella Mae knew someone was about to enter. The sound of heavy boots on the wooden boardwalk out front had abruptly stopped, and Colonel, the orange calico cat that lived in the store, raised himself from a nap on the store's counter.

From where she sat in an upholstered chair in front of an unlit fireplace in the adjoining drawing room, a hurricane lamp providing light by which she could sew, Ella Mae furrowed her blonde brows. The cat's hair was puffed out in all directions, making him appear nearly double his normal size.

She stood and hurried to the counter, closing the curtain separating the store from the drawing room. Her father occasionally used it as a sitting room, the scents of pipe tobacco, musk, and wood smoke still lingering in the air.

When a young man appeared wearing a flannel shirt, loose tubular trousers held up with suspenders, and a groom's cap, Colonel immediately settled back onto the counter and apparently resumed his nap. The distinctive odor of horse filled the air.

Setting aside the lengths of fabric she had been stitching together, Ella Mae greeted the customer. "Good morning, sir. May I be of any assistance?" Her eyes rounded slightly when she recognized John O'Connor. He was several inches taller and his shoulders seemed broader than the last time she had seen him seated at one of the desks in the back row of the schoolroom they had shared most of their lives. Gossip about town suggested he was working for Mr. Perkins at the local stable, a recent development given the owner was suffering with consumption and might not live long. "Mr. O'Connor. It's good to see you again."

John lifted his cap and gave her a nod. "Miss Montgomery," he acknowledged. He clutched his cap in both hands while he regarded Colonel as if the cat might attack him. With his attention on the feline, it gave Ella Mae a moment to realize why she hadn't immediately recognized him.

He wore an eye patch over one eye.

She was sure he didn't sport it the last time she had seen him, but that had been a couple of years ago.

"What are you in need of on this fine day?" she asked.

"I'm looking for bridles. Tack. Stuff for horses," the young man replied. Although there was a hint of an accent sounding in his words, Ella Mae knew he hadn't come to Galena directly from Ireland. He was easy to understand, and he wasn't as pale as those who arrived from the Emerald Isle seeking a better life in America. His father had been an immigrant, though, a laborer who helped build the Illinois and Michigan Canal and had died the year before.

"Did they not have what you needed down at Grant's leather goods store?" she asked, stepping from behind the counter. Jesse Grant's son, Ulysses, had moved to Galena only the year before to work as a clerk in the store, but once the South threatened to leave the Union, his military experience saw him commissioned a colonel of the 21st Illinois Volunteer Infantry Regiment. Although she had never been in the two-story brick structure while he clerked there, she had heard he wasn't much of a salesman, preferring instead to talk about the Mexican War with anyone who would listen.

"I... I didn't look there," John stammered. "Your store is closer to the stable," he added, waving to the Galena Stable across the street. "Can't afford to be away too long."

Ella Mae sensed there was something odd about his manner, but decided he had a point. The leather goods store was several blocks down the street. "There are a few bridles back here," she said, leading him to a rack upon which several leather bridles and leads hung from hooks. "They're not real fancy, though."

"Thanks," he said, his attention on her until she glanced at him. She was sure he was blushing as he regarded the tack with a critical eye. "Don't need fancy, these'll do."

"Did Mr. Perkins acquire another pair of horses?" Ella Mae asked, well aware the beasts were in high demand for the war effort.

"Something like that. The ones he sold to a general last month required they come with tack," he explained. "I made what I could with what leather we had, but…" He let the sentence trail off as he shrugged.

"I'll let Father know to order more, if you'd like," she offered. "We get them in on the steamship from St. Louis."

"Appreciate it. I'm probably going to buy all of these."

Ella Mae's eyes rounded. "All right. I'll be at the front when you're ready to pay," she said, sure he was watching her as she walked away from him. She was half-tempted to add some extra sway to her hips—she'd seen her mother do it a hundred times with her father—but she wasn't sure she should be flirting with the mysterious John O'Connor.

Returning to her sewing, Ella Mae hummed softly as she finished stitching a seam. Creating the bodice and sleeves of a gown never took her long. It was the skirt that seemed to take forever, the yards and yards of fabric difficult to negotiate as she sewed the seams together with tiny, even stitches. The hem seemed to take even longer. With the change in fashion from the decade prior, a gown's skirts were so wide, they required a crinoline to hold them in their dome shape. Ella had already seen evidence that future gowns wouldn't have the same silhouette, though. The latest fashion journals from New York were showing narrower skirts with the volume moving to the posterior.

She couldn't decide if she was looking forward to that particular change or not.

"I think these will do me for now," John said as he joined her at the counter. He spread out three bridles and a number of leads on the polished wood, careful to avoid bothering the cat.

"Colonel doesn't bite," Ella remarked. "But he does take up entirely too much space."

As if he understood her words, Colonel lifted his head, yawned, and jumped down from the counter.

"I think he's taken offense to your assessment of his size," John commented, a grin lifting the corner of his mouth. A dimple appeared to dent his lower cheek, which softened a face that appeared somewhat menacing due to the eye patch.

"He can take all the offense he wants, but he knows it's true. Besides, I'm the one who usually feeds him, so…" She shrugged.

Apparently Colonel was rubbing one of John's legs,

because he glanced down and said, "I could use a cat like you. A good mouser, no doubt?"

"He is," Ella affirmed, dipping a pen into an ink pot so she could write out the receipt. "As are the others who have adopted us over the years." She handed him the receipt. "You must have acquired more than a pair of horses," she commented, waving to the bridles.

"In a manner of speaking," he replied. He handed over some bills, and Ella Mae made the change from the cash register. "I'm seeing to the Galena Stable, since Mr. Perkins is too sick to do it any longer."

Ella Mae sighed softly. "I heard he was ill, but I didn't realize it was that bad," she remarked.

John lifted a shoulder. "'Fraid so." He paused a moment. "Do you suppose... would you ever agree to take a ride with me about town?"

"On a horse?" she asked, surprised by the query.

"I... I was thinking in a carriage of some sort," he clarified.

"Oh," she breathed. "I suppose I would. If it was all right with my Father," she added, her heart suddenly racing.

He appeared to be about to say something, but instead merely nodded.

"Would you like me to wrap these in paper for you?" she asked, curious as to what he had been about to say.

He furrowed a brow. "Uh… that won't be necessary," he replied. He inhaled and nodded to the pieces of fabric she had set aside. "May I ask what it is you're making?"

Ella Mae grinned. "A ballgown," she said proudly. "Mother says I can go to this year's masquerade ball at the DeSoto House Hotel."

"I saw mention of it in the *Galena Gazette*," he commented.

"It will be my come-out," she stated proudly.

He gave a start. "Come-out?" he repeated, as if he hadn't heard the word before.

"My introduction to Society," she clarified.

He seemed momentarily confused. "I... I would have thought you were already out in Society."

She tittered. "I feel as if I am. My mother's friends include me when they invite her to tea, but... this will be my first formal ball. Not like the dances at the hall," she explained.

"Oh. So... so you'll be looking for suitors whilst you're there?"

She gave a start. "Oh. I'll mostly be hoping for dance partners," she replied, knowing full well her cheeks were bright pink. "I've no idea what to expect." She had a thought that perhaps John might attend the affair. "I suppose I wouldn't be adverse to gaining a suitor from the experience. Should... someone... be... interested," she stammered.

He seemed to think on her response for a moment. "If it's a masquerade ball, doesn't that mean you'll be wearing a mask?"

She nodded.

"So… how would a gentleman know who you are? So he can become a suitor?"

Inhaling to answer, Ella Mae resisted the urge to giggle. "I've absolutely no idea. So… I suppose introductions will be required, although I can't imagine the bit of lace I'll be wearing as a mask will hide much of my face. I'm going as an angel, you see."

He regarded her with an odd expression before finally nodding. "Well, I expect your dance card will be full. Good day, Miss Montgomery."

"Good day, Mr. O'Connor."

Ella Mae watched him go, sure her face was still bright pink. Why was it John O'Conor had her feeling as if she had made a fool of herself?

CHAPTER 2
AN ANNIVERSARY DAY

*E*arlier that morning

For a moment, Ella Mae secretly wished she hadn't had to work at the store that day. Usually her father, Robert Montgomery, would be at the counter, but he and her mother were off on a trip to nearby Dubuque. "We're celebrating our wedding anniversary," her mother had explained before they had departed. "I find it hard to believe your father and I have been married nineteen years."

Resisting the urge to roll her eyes, Ella Mae had been tempted to remind her mother she would be nineteen on her next birthday, even if it was nine months away. "Why not go out for a fancy dinner at the DeSoto House Hotel instead?" she had asked.

She was sure her mother blushed three shades of pink and red before she stammered something about eating a later dinner at the hotel would be as unnerving as leaving their children home alone after dark.

How many nights had they already done so in the past few years? Evenings when Ella Mae had been charged with seeing to her younger brother, Bobby, while Mrs. Jackson, their housekeeper and cook, saw to everything else?

"Especially given the... the *hauntings*," Emma said, arching a blonde brow to emphasize her point.

That comment had certainly caused a stir, especially because her father and Bobby had stepped into the house right in time to overhear it. They had been out in the carriage house seeing to hitching the horse to their curricle.

"Hauntings?" Bobby had repeated in alarm. Despite his age of only twelve, the boy had shot up in height during the past year so that he was nearly as tall as his mother.

"*Another* report of a ghost?" Robert added, scoffing with humor.

Ella Mae hadn't yet decided if she believed in ghosts or not, but the tales of sightings throughout the town of Galena had the townsfolk either entertained or on edge.

"The jail again, darling," Emma replied, rushing to kiss her husband on the cheek. "I'm nearly ready. Do you suppose I'll need a heavier coat?"

"Not on this day," he replied. "It feels as if summer doesn't want to give way to autumn out there. I need to change my shirt, and I'll be right with you." He hurried up the stairs of their three-story house in Prospect Street. Before he disappeared, he added, "Oh, and we're going to drop off Bobby at Sumner's place."

"Oh?" Emma had asked, a look of worry crossing her face.

"Mr. Sumner said he has a job for me today," Bobby claimed with excitement. "Said he'll pay me fifty cents to help him unload the wagons." That morning's train from Freeport, part of the Illinois Central Railroad, had deposited a number of passengers, some intending to live and work in Galena while others were on their way West to claim the one-hundred and sixty acres of land afforded by the Homestead Act. In addition to people, the train carried a number of crates, boxes, and the U.S. mail, which required delivery to their final destinations. Most of the freight had been loaded onto wagons that were being pulled by draft horses to several destinations along Main Street.

"My shoes and wings," Ella Mae had said with excitement. In September, she had mailed an order for the dance slippers to a shoemaker in Illinois' largest city with the hope they would arrive in time for the ball. As part of her father's regular order for the dry goods store, she had begged him to include a set of wings suitable for a costume.

"My glazes," Emma had said at the same time. As a potter of both utilitarian pots and decorative pieces,

Emma had moved from Stoke-on-Trent in England two decades prior and settled in Galena to practice her craft and consign her wares in local stores. Montgomery Dry Goods was the first to stock her red clay pottery, and not long after, she and Robert were married. "So he wouldn't have to pay me for my pots any longer," Emma had said when Ella Mae asked how they had come to be married.

His cats at the time, General and Admiral, had acted as matchmakers, their mischief responsible for not only breaking every pot already for sale in the store, but also in seeing to it Emma returned to Montgomery Dry Goods to act as a nurse. Robert had suffered a cut to his hand whilst cleaning up the pottery shards, and his wound required stitches.

Emma had seen to the stitches as well as some kisses and other measures to assist in the healing process.

Marriage wasn't far behind.

The current generations of General and Admiral were curled up near the front door, their large orange bodies angled to absorb as much of the morning's autumnal light as was streaming in through the side window.

"Thank you for covering the store today," Emma commented.

Ella Mae shrugged. "I'm happy to do it."

"We'll try to be home before noon tomorrow, so do see to locking up the store and the house tonight," her mother continued. "Mrs. Jackson will be here to make supper and breakfast for you and your brother," she added. "If you should need anything, pay a call on Mrs. Sumner." Beatrice Sumner had been her first pottery customer in Galena, buying the more decorative items Emma created on her pottery wheel.

"I have my gown to work on if it's slow at the store," Ella Mae had said, wondering at her mother's growing nervousness.

"I've never been much of a seamstress, so I'm glad Mrs. Watkins took you under her wing and taught you so much about sewing," Emma remarked, retrieving a valise from the bottom of the stairs. "She says she'll have my gown finished in time for the ball." Although Alice Watkins didn't claim to be a modiste, she had been making gowns for Emma since her arrival in Galena twenty years prior.

"What about your mask?" Ella Mae asked.

Emma shrugged. "I expect a bit of lace will do the trick. It's not as if I'm having my come-out."

"Ah, but since you never had one, we can pretend it is," Robert said in his slight Irish brogue as he descended the stairs. A whiff of his cologne, amber mixed with spice and a hint of citrus, wafted past Ella Mae's nose. "Sweep you off your feet and into my equipage," he continued, grabbing his wife's hand as he headed for the front door.

General and Admiral both uncurled and stood as they passed, followed by Bobby and finally by Ella Mae, who resisted rolling her eyes as she closed and locked the door behind her. Only one of the cats returned to his nap, blissfully unaware of what was about to happen that day.

Or perhaps he knew full well.

As for the other, well, "mischief" might have been his other name.

CHAPTER 3
A MAN BOTHERED

A few minutes later, Galena Stable

"Perfect," John murmured, unaware he had said the word out loud.

She was, though. Perfect. Even when they'd been in the same schoolroom, year after year.

Miss Ella Mae Montgomery. Blonde, with eyes the color of the cornflowers that grew wild along the banks of the Galena River. A voice with the barest hint of a British accent, as if she had been born to an aristocrat and was trying to hide it. Her manner wasn't the least bit condescending, though. Not like some of the townsfolk who kept their horses at the stable and still treated him as he were the boy he was when he had left Galena to join the war effort the year before. He had returned a grown man, his eye injury from an errant gunshot preventing him from continuing his service in the Union army.

He supposed they couldn't help that their small town, which only two decades prior featured a single church, a few stores, and a nightlife consisting of laborers and miners getting drunk at the local tavern, had grown into a full-fledged town with over a dozen churches, at least fifty businesses, and who knew how many taverns. Despite the destruction caused by the fires of 1854 and 1856 along Main Street, the businesses had all been rebuilt, although not with wood. Social functions, such as the upcoming masquerade ball, enlivened the city several days every month.

Galena was a far cry from the town his father had come to forty years ago to mine lead and to work as a laborer on the canal.

Whatever in the world had brought Miss Ella Mae Montgomery's mother to such a backwater, he had no idea. But what had Ella Mae been doing since she completed school? Working in her father's dry goods store? She had looked as radiant as the white-on-white roses in the fabric she was stitching when he had arrived. Although most in town spoke of the war and nothing else, she behaved as if she didn't have a care in the world.

Perhaps she didn't. Perhaps being the daughter of a store owner was secure enough that she didn't have to worry about war or money. She certainly wouldn't have to resort to prostitution to make her living, nor was spinsterhood in her future.

At least, not according to her father.

Even if John didn't know otherwise, he knew it was

unlikely she would remain an unmarried woman for long. At least, not around Galena. Due to the lead mines, men outnumbered women. Or rather, they had. With the war on and so many young—and older—men off to join the Union forces, the numbers might have evened out a bit.

That was obviously why Robert Montgomery had come to the stable the day before and asked for a moment of his time. The man's concern for his daughter's future had been the topic of their brief conversation. Before he knew it, John was nodding his head, promising he would at least consider her father's proposition.

A plaintive '*meow*' sounded from below, and John glanced down to discover an orange calico cat at his feet. "Colonel?" he asked in surprise.

The cat purred and rubbed his body against John's legs.

"Uh, you need to get back to your store," he said. "Before you're missed." He moved to the first stall, where one of four carriage horses had been left by its owner earlier that morning. Exchanged with other horses owned by the same railroad baron, the matched set would remain until the gentleman passed through town again in a week or so.

He began brushing the bay, one of his hands resting on its withers as he worked. A thought of brushing Ella Mae's hair came to mind, the long blonde hair shining with his every stroke. He wasn't actually sure how long her locks were—she always wore her hair in a bun atop her head, a pair of bouncy ringlets framing her face—but he was imagining it past her shoulders. If she was lying in his bed, her head on the pillow, he was sure the golden blonde locks would be splayed out, making her appear angelic. Instead of the horse's quiet knickers, he heard Ella Mae's sighs of satisfaction.

He thought of her long fingers as they took the tiny stitches in the white fabric, as they smoothed the wrinkles from the material. Thought of her fingernails, perfect ovals, how they would feel should she spear them through his dark hair and scrape his scalp. He involuntarily shuddered, his eyes closing at experiencing what he was thinking.

An image flashed before his mind's eye of her stroking his skin with her fingers. Of her hands smoothing down his chest, over his stomach, and down through the dark curls surrounding his manhood. Of one of those hands gripping it, rubbing it until it was hard and ready for release.

John blinked and dropped his head back, a soft curse sounding when he realized how uncomfortable his nether region had become with his carnal thoughts. The horse suddenly turned to regard him with a look of annoyance, and John realized he had stopped brushing the beast. "Sorry," he said, resuming his work.

His thoughts quickly returned to Ella Mae, to the gown she was making for the masquerade ball at the DeSoto House Hotel. Mrs. Watkins had mentioned it when she had come for her daily ride earlier that morning. She seemed insistent he attend the ball. "Young men will be lacking in numbers," she had explained. "And young ladies like Miss Ella Mae Montgomery will be so disappointed if there aren't enough men with whom to dance."

Was it possible he could obtain a ticket to the ball? Dress in his Sunday best and claim a dance or two on Miss Montgomery's dance card?

It's a masquerade ball, he reminded himself. His Sunday best wouldn't be required. A costume of some sort would be, though. As for a mask, he probably didn't require one. He already wore an eye patch.

Did he even remember how to dance? His mother, God bless her, had done her best to teach him when he was a boy of fourteen. She had died a year later, and she had never seen him dance in public.

John had nearly talked himself out of attending the ball when he felt Colonel rubbing against his legs again. Scoffing, he set aside the brush, bent, and picked up the cat. "Time to take you back where you belong," he said, cradling the calico against his shoulder.

He half expected the cat would object and try to escape his hold, but instead, Colonel purred loudly as John made his way back to Montgomery Dry Goods. He grinned at feeling the vibration through his shirt and waistcoat, and once again he imagined being in a bed with Ella Mae. Would she purr like Colonel when he pleasured her? Purr with satisfaction whilst he held her body against the front of his ? Purr when he kissed her?

Glad he carried a cat—no one would notice the bulge in his trousers given the orange calico—he found Miss Ella Mae sewing at the counter, an orange cat curled up near where she worked.

"Why, hello again, Mr. O'Connor," she said brightly, displaying a huge grin when she noticed he carried a cat.

"Hello," he replied, stunned at seeing the cat who lounged next to where she worked. "I was thinking to return your cat, but..." He motioned to the one on the counter. "I see you're not missing one."

Setting aside her sewing, she giggled. "Sergeant, you naughty boy," she said, coming from behind the counter to lift the orange cat from his hold. "I wondered where he'd gotten off to," she added, directing her attention to John.

For a moment, John wished *his* name was Sergeant. The thought of being her naughty boy held more appeal than it should have. "He... he was in the stable. I thought..." He pointed to Colonel. "I thought it was him."

She rolled her eyes. "I'm so sorry if he was a pest. He's the worst of all of them, though."

"All of them?" John repeated. He really should be getting back to the stable, but stealing another moment with the delectable Ella Mae surely wouldn't hurt.

"There are four of them. That we know of," she replied, dumping Sergeant onto the counter to join his brother, Colonel. "Admiral and General are the others. As for if they're *ours*, well, do cats ever actually belong to anyone? I've always had the impression *we* belong to *them*."

He chuckled softly. "Is that why one is named General? Because you report to him?"

A musical laugh sounded from Ella Mae. When he grinned in response, a dimple appeared at the base of his cheek. "He is in charge," she remarked. "They all are, truth be told," she agreed.

"Ah," he replied, grinning "And I suppose they all look the same?"

She tittered. "Almost exactly," she agreed. "The older two were litter mates, and these two... well, they are probably General's sons."

The bell on the front door tinkled, and John gave a start. "Oh, pardon me. I… I need to be getting back to the stable," he said, wincing at the thought of having to leave her.

"Of course. Thank you for returning Sergeant," she said. "Naughty boy," she said again, directing her comment to the cat.

John tipped his cap and took his leave, stepping around the two matrons who had just arrived.

Naughty boy. He struggled to keep a straight face as he made his way across the street.

He was unaware of the orange fur ball that escaped the shop along with him.

CHAPTER 4
A TRYST

eanwhile, in a third-story room at the *DeSoto House Hotel*

"I cannot decide if you are fascinated by my bosom or with my gown," Emma said, angling her head to one side as she regarded her fifty-three-year-old husband with an arched brow.

Robert jerked out of his reverie, the words exactly the same as those she had said to him the first day they had met. He remembered how her gown had him worried someone had set up another dry goods store in Galena without his knowledge. How her British accent had intrigued him. How it had him believing she was high-born.

"Uh…" He chuckled softly. "Of course I was staring at your bosom, my lady," he admitted. He rushed to gather her into his arms. "I hope you you know I'm going to spend this entire day ravishing you in this…"

He turned to take in the bed in the small hotel room, his brows furrowing at seeing it was no larger than the one in their master bedchamber. "This poor excuse for a bed," he finished.

Emma tittered. "Whatever had you thinking we should spend our anniversary *here*?" she asked, moving to undo the buttons of his sack jacket. "And telling the children we were going to Dubuque of all places?"

"I wanted us to do something… different," he replied, glancing down to see she was already undoing his waistcoat buttons.

"I thought we'd all be going to St. Louis," she said, giving him a pointed glance as she pushed the garments from his shoulders.

"Next year. For our twentieth anniversary," he promised, turning her around so he could undo the fastenings of her gown. He could feel the crinolines beneath her bell skirt press against his legs. "By then, perhaps you won't have to wear hoop skirts," he added hopefully. He had seen what was to come in the way of ladies' fashion, and he was looking forward to a time when the large bell skirts would go the way of panniers.

She giggled. "I am not looking forward to my bottom appearing as if I'm bent over and sticking it out as I make my way down Main Street," she argued, turning around to undo the knot of his neck cloth.

"You can continue to wear your current gowns. I shall not mind," he replied, although he made sure he didn't sound enthusiastic about the prospect.

A quelling glance was her first response. "Why does that not surprise me?"

"You could wear nothing at all, and I wouldn't mind a bit," he whispered, his lips feathering over her forehead and down to her cheek and then to her lips.

"I'd be covered in red clay when I leave my studio," she argued.

"I would bathe you," he offered, a brow arching in a tease.

She giggled as her gown fell to the floor. "Robert Michael Montgomery," she said, feigning indignation.

"I love it when you scold me," he murmured, undoing the ties of her crinoline and her corset before lifting her chemise from her body. His gaze darted to the floor. He half expected a cat to come out from under her gown. The large calicos seemed to favor hiding beneath her hoops.

"I hardly know why," she countered, her blonde brows once again arching.

He cleared his throat. "It reminds me that I can occasionally behave in an improper manner and still expect you to sleep in the same bed with me." From her widened eyes, Robert realized she had anticipated a different answer. "What?" he asked, all innocence.

"I am rather glad you agreed to feature my pottery in your shop all those years ago," she stated.

He blinked. "How could I not? General saw to it all the pots I had on the shelves were destroyed," he claimed.

She dipped her head but regarded him through the curtain of his lashes. "Despite the injuries you sustained as a result of that debacle, you didn't seem to mind." She reached for the hand where she'd had to stitch up the nasty cut, the scar from six stitches still visible in the middle of his palm.

Nodding, he pulled her into his arms. "Not a bit," he admitted. "I think I fell in love with you the moment you stepped into my store that day," he claimed.

"I certainly didn't get that impression," she countered. If anything, she had thought he was annoyed by her visit. A woman speaking with a British accent and implying his pottery wares were substandard, even if they were and he knew it. Or perhaps it had been her calling card, the elegant white pasteboard engraved in black.

Avalon Pottery
Premiere pottery in the style of England's finest
Emma Avalon, Proprietress

He had even had the audacity to suggest she was from D.A. Sackett and Co. The Dewey Street pottery manufacturer hadn't produced a single utilitarian pot at that point, but once they did, she'd had competition. Eschewing creating utilitarian pots in favor of more decorative ceramics, the sales of the finer creations proved she had made the right choice. Her wares were a popular product in Montgomery Dry Goods.

"Lust, then?" he prompted.

She tittered. "I suppose I can believe that," she admitted, remembering how it hadn't been long after she had stitched his wound before they had kissed. A few minutes later, they had rushed up to his rooms above the store and were frantically undressing one another.

"I wish to make love to you, Mrs. Montgomery."

Glancing down between them, she realized he was still wearing his shirt, trousers, and black shoes. His trousers were tented where his manhood jutted out from his body. "Well, then I suppose I need to divest you of the rest of your clothes," she replied.

He was quick to move to the edge of the bed, leaning against it as he removed his shoes and then pushed his trousers from his body.

In the meantime, Emma lifted her gown from the floor and tossed it over the back of a chair, giving a start when Admiral darted out from beneath the crinoline and hid under the bed.

Robert heard her scoff and paused whilst undoing the buttons at his wrists. "What is it?"

Emma's gaze went from the carpeted floor to him. "Uh, nothing, but I do believe I need to see to your shirt," she said, lifting the linen garment from his torso. "Mr. Montgomery," she breathed.

"Yes, Mrs. Montgomery?" he responded, glancing down between their bodies.

"The time for talk seems to have come to an end." She arched a brow.

Robert lowered his face, his lips capturing hers in a

scorching kiss at the same time one of his hands smoothed down the side of her body to the globes of her bottom.

When he briefly pulled away to take a much needed breath, Emma murmured, "Actually, I should say one more thing."

"Oh?" he muttered, kissing her cheeks and then the side of her neck down to her shoulder.

"We're not alone."

In the middle of kissing the top of her shoulder, he paused. Straightening, he glanced around the room. "Did you… did you see a ghost?"

She gave him a quelling glance. "Something like that," she whispered. "Admiral is under the bed."

Robert blinked. "How?"

"He was hiding under my skirts."

Rolling his eyes, Robert was about to scold the cat but decided it wasn't worth it. If it hadn't been Admiral, it would have been General. The two felines seemed to take turns making mischief. "He's the luckiest creature on the planet," he commented.

Emma rubbed her bare breasts against his chest, the tips of her nipples parting the whorls of dark hair. "Even now?"

Robert inhaled sharply. "It's my turn to be the luckiest," he whispered, pushing her back until the bed was directly behind her. Lifting her bottom, he had her seated on the edge, her legs wrapped around his hips as his manhood sought her opening. "Apologies, but I really need you right now," he whispered. He thrust into her and let out a groan of satisfaction.

Admiral *meowed* loudly, and Emma tittered as she supported herself on her elbows.

Cursing softly, Robert thrust into her again, which had her quickly sobering. She dropped back onto the bed and moaned as he placed a thumb where their bodies met, his thrusts increasing in speed and intensity. When she gasped—his ministrations had her experiencing a sharp and pleasurable orgasm—he growled with his own release. A moment later, he collapsed atop her. Between labored breaths, he asked if she was all right.

"I'm perfect," she purred. "And it will be perfection when we're actually *in* this bed," she hinted, grinning.

Admiral purred loudly from where he sat at the end of the bed.

"Purrfection, indeed," Robert murmured.

CHAPTER 5
MATCHMAKERS ATTEMPT A MATCH

eanwhile, inside Montgomery Dry Goods Ella Mae rolled her eyes when she realized Sergeant had jumped down from the counter and was probably no longer in the store. He had no doubt followed Mr. O'Connor out at the same moment Mrs. Beatrice Sumner and Mrs. Alice Watkins had entered.

The two were probably concerned about her running the store alone, given her parents were out of town. "Morning, ladies," she said brightly.

"Good morning to you," Beatrice replied, waggling her eyebrows. "I take it our plan worked?" she asked with excitement, her gloved hands balled into fists as she shook them on either side of her shoulders.

Ella Mae blinked. "Plan?" she repeated.

Alice joined them at the counter. "Well, did he ask you?"

Befuddled, Ella Mae's attention darted between the two women. "Ask me what?"

"If he could escort you," they said in unison.

"Escort me… where?"

The two huffed. "To the masquerade ball, of course," Alice replied, sounding exasperated.

"Or at least to reserve two dances on your card for him," Beatrice put in.

Ella Mae lifted a shoulder. "No, and… no," she replied before her face screwed into a grimace. "What have you done?" She was sure she was displaying several shades of red at learning they had said something to the poor groom. Had John O'Connor come into the shop and bought the bridles simply because the older women had encouraged him to seek some dances with her?

The two matrons exchanged quick glances. "Well, apparently nothing of note," Alice said with a huff.

"Did my mother put you up to this?" Ella Mae asked, suspicion evident in her voice. Despite their age difference—Beatrice was at least a decade older than her mother—Beatrice and Emma Montgomery had been friends since Emma's arrival in Galena.

"She had nothing to do with this," Beatrice assured her. "This is entirely your fa—"

"*Our* doing," Alice interrupted.

Ella Mae's gaze darted between the two women. "To what end?" she gingerly asked.

"Well, courtship, of course," Beatrice replied. "John O'Connor is of an age to be married, as are you, and now that he's in charge of the stable, he has steady employment."

"And he won't be going off to fight in the war," Alice chimed in.

The reminder of war had Ella Mae wincing. The year before, it seemed as if half of Galena's unattached male population had left town to don the Union uniform and fight for the North. Many others who sided with the South had also left with the intent to wear the gray uniform.

But she knew as well as the two matrons that the real reason John O'Connor hadn't gone off to war was because of his eye.

Or perhaps he had, and he'd been injured in one of the early battles. Perhaps that's why Ella Mae hadn't seen him about town since their days in the schoolroom had ended.

"I appreciate your efforts, I really do," Ella Mae said. "But I rather doubt Mr. O'Connor will be attending the masquerade ball."

The two matrons exchanged looks of frustration before Beatrice pulled a list from her pocket. "Oh, all right," she said in resignation. "If you could see to it this order is ready by four o'clock, I'll have Mr. Sumner pick it up." She left a basket on the counter. "He should be done with deliveries from the train by then."

Ella Mae read the list and nodded. "I'll have these items pulled and ready before then," she promised.

She bade the two a good day and went about filling

the order. As she did so, bits of her conversation with John O'Connor flashed before her mind's eye.

He had so rarely spoken whilst they were in school, she had been surprised upon hearing his first words that morning. She had detected a hint of an Irish brogue in his voice, his manner of speech so much like her father's. That would explain his dark, nearly black hair and those sapphire blue eyes.

"Black Irish," she murmured, barely aware she said the words out loud. "Too handsome for his own good. No wonder the horses like him." She rolled her eyes when she realized she was talking to herself, but she didn't wish to stop thinking of Mr. O'Connor and his rugged appearance. The eye patch merely added a hint of mystery.

Like most men in town, he had no qualms about showing his forearms, for his sleeves had been rolled up past his elbows. The flannel work shirt had done nothing to hide the width of his shoulders or the breadth of his chest or the circumference of his upper arms. Upon her first sight of him, she had noticed how his muscles bulged beneath the fabric, as if they were attempting to escape.

He could probably lift her with one arm. Lift her up against a wall and hold her there whilst he had his way with her.

She couldn't recall another man in Galena having such a physique. At least not among those who worked on Main Street. "Probably from working with horses.

Lifting saddles, and bales of hay, and you're talking to yourself again." She rolled her eyes. One of the side effects of being alone in the shop, she supposed.

She tried to concentrate on the next item on the scrap of paper she held, Mrs. Sumner's list neatly printed in black ink.

Gauze strips.

A shiver ran down Ella Mae's spine at the thought of Mr. O'Connor stripping her bare. Of how his hands would feel skimming over her warm skin. Of how his palm would feel holding one of her breasts, his thumb caressing a nipple until it was tight with need.

Need of *what*, she wasn't quite sure, but if she kept this up, she would be in need of a new pair of drawers. She had grown damp at at the apex of her thighs, all because she couldn't get her mind off of John O'Connor.

Think of Mother, she thought. Think of what she'd had to do to be the best potter in town.

Her gaze darted to one of the vases Emma Avalon Montgomery had made the week before in her small studio at their house on Prospect Street. Her kiln, moved from her original house in Galena, was now in the back garden. Every week, her newest creations were fired, usually three times, before they appeared on the display shelves at Montgomery Dry Goods.

Ella Mae's grandfather, Edward Avalon, had been a master at creating beautiful stoneware, an expert at shaping clay on a potters' wheel, a scientist when it came to firing the earthenware, and an artist with the tiny brushes needed to create idyllic country scenes on the sides of pots and the petals of English roses on vases.

Everything Ella Mae's mother knew about pottery she had learned from her father. Everything she had owned prior to marrying Robert Montgomery had been due to what *he* had created.

Well, and because Great Aunt Adeline had been generous in her last will and testament. She had seen to it that Emma inherited what she hadn't spent on her worldly travels and extensive wardrobe. That meant Ella Mae's parents' initial few years of marriage hadn't required they live in poverty as so many other newlyweds in Galena were forced to do. They had been able to build a house in Prospect Street. Furnish it with fine furniture from St. Louis. Hire a cook and housekeeper, and later a nanny to see to the children.

Ella Mae knew she had led a privileged life, for the girls with whom she had attended school were frequently daughters of the lead miners or those who worked on the canal or in the shipping industry. As for the boys, they were much the same, many dropping out of school before they had reached the last grade in order to work or to help in their families' businesses.

John O'Connor had been one of those boys. Quiet and apparently shy, he had always sat in the last row in the classroom. "Son of a laborer who's digging the canal," one of her friends had commented, when they noticed how he always headed straight for home when school was done for the day.

She hadn't seen him since her days in a schoolroom had ended.

So where had he been?

With a sudden rush of customers, Ella Mae was forced to concentrate on business for the rest of the day. Even so, thoughts of John had her wishing he might return to the store, sooner rather than later.

CHAPTER 6
A RIDE HOME

*L*ater that day

At six o'clock, Ella Mae folded up her sewing into a basket and took one last look around the store before she stepped outside. As she turned to lock the door, an image of John once again flashed before her mind's eye, and the oddest sensation rushed down her spine. Flutterbies danced about in her stomach, and frissons of pleasure skittered beneath her skin.

Inhaling softly, Ella Mae paused a moment before she turned to head east.

She nearly collided with John O'Connor.

Giving a start, she stared up at him. Had she conjured him into existence with her thoughts?

"Oh, pardon me, Mr. O'Connor." She stepped back and curtsied. "I did not see you there."

The expression on the man's face was by no means

pleasant. In fact, the stablehand looked as if he had worked himself into some sort of rage, his face red and his fists on his hips.

"Why, whatever is wrong, Mr. O"Connor?" she asked, her eyes widening in fright. "Was something wrong with the bridles?" The patch he wore over one eye made him appear far too menacing.

"Where do you think you're going, my lady?"

Ella Mae blinked and glanced about. "Well, home, sir. It's after six o'clock."

His expression grew more fearsome—if that was even possible. "Alone?"

She shook her head. "Oh, goodness, no. My father arranged a ride for me. He said I'm to go to the lobby of the DeSoto House Hotel, and someone I know would be there to drive me home."

John's fierce expression softened. "Oh. Uh..." He swallowed and briefly closed his eye. "Forgive me. I feared you were intending to walk home by yourself," he muttered.

Ella Mae scoffed with indignation. "Not with the lead miners coming into town for their ales," she replied. There weren't nearly as many of them now as there had been before the California Gold Rush—those who had left did so for the prospect of a better life, and with the war, even fewer were left to work in the mines. Still, it was never safe to be out after dark unescorted.

Even in the golden hour, when the sun was setting and the downtown was cast in a wash of yellow light to match the leaves on most of the trees, Ella Mae could see the stablehand was embarrassed. "Would you care to walk with me to the hotel so I won't be alone?"

He glanced toward the stable. "Uh, of course." He didn't offer an arm but merely walked beside her as they made their way. "About the masquerade ball," he said suddenly.

"Yes?" she responded, hiding the surprise she felt at hearing him bring up the topic. "Have you decided to attend?"

"I'll be there," he stated. "Seeing as how I already have a mask of sorts." He lifted a hand to indicate his eye patch.

She resisted the urge to grin. "Ah, but what costume will you wear to go with it? Will you be a pirate, perhaps? Or a—"

"I was thinking I could be a highwayman," he stated, arching his brow as if he was waiting for her reaction.

A frisson passed through Ella Mae, and she knew he heard her inhalation of breath. "You would wear a black cloak over all black clothes and carry... what? A gun and a riding crop?" She wasn't sure why she felt excitement at imagining him in such an outfit.

"Probably not the gun," he replied, humor sounding in his voice. They had nearly reached the DeSoto, and he indicated an old phaeton parked in front. "Your carriage awaits, my lady," he said, bowing slightly as he held out his arm to indicate the black equipage hitched to a Bay.

Ella Mae stared at him a moment before her

attention went to the front doors of the DeSoto House Hotel and back to him. Is that why he had asked if she would agree to go on a ride with him? Except... "My father arranged for *you* to give me a ride home?" she asked in surprise.

"He even paid me," he replied dryly. "Although I can't think why *he* isn't driving you himself."

"Oh, that's because he and my mother have gone to Dubuque for their wedding anniversary," she explained, her attention on the phaeton. She didn't notice him screw up his face in confusion.

"Huh," he murmured.

Doing her best not to keep her mouth from dropping open, she continued to regard the phaeton and then the horse with a look of uncertainty. "I've never ridden on one of these," she said, attempting to quell her nervousness. A phaeton required the riders to sit on a bench. A rather small bench. At least this one had a pole she could cling to whilst they negotiated corners, for otherwise she was quite sure she would slide off the bench and end up on her bum in the street.

"Would you like some help?" he asked, taking the sewing basket from her. He stowed it on the back of the phaeton, in a rack large enough for a small trunk.

She glanced up first at him and then at the two steps required to reach the bench. Given the crinoline beneath her skirt, she wasn't sure how she would manage climbing the steep steps.

Moving to stand in front of her, he asked, "Do you trust me?"

Ella Mae stared up at him, "Um." Before she could finish forming a coherent response, he had his hands at her waist and was lifting her onto the bench. Neither of them noticed the cat that darted out from beneath her skirts and jumped onto the back of the phaeton.

"Oh!" she cried out in surprise. Before she could put voice to a protest, she was seated on the bench, clinging to the pole with one hand as she pulled her skirts into some semblance of order. She was about to scold John, but he was already making his way around the front of the horse to the driver's side of the phaeton.

When he hopped up onto the bench, he gave a her a nod and took the reins in hand. A moment later, they were off and turning right onto Green Street.

Neither of them noticed the silhouette of the man who watched from a third-story window above, his body mostly hidden by the drapes.

"I'm not really a lady," she said suddenly, once they were headed up the slight hill.

"I beg your pardon?" he responded, barely turning to regard her.

"You keep saying, 'my lady', as if I'm a daughter of an aristocrat or someone important. But I am not."

He chuckled softly. "I suppose I say it because you sound like one. Or at least, what I think one might sound like. All proper and such, like your mother."

Ella Mae tried to discern if he thought her mother's

British accent made her sound better than the other ladies in the town. "I don't mean to put on airs," she argued, thinking that might be his point.

"I didn't say you did." He finally glanced over at her. "You're just very ladylike."

Giving him a prim grin, she relaxed despite the death grip she employed as she hung onto the pole. "You sound like my father."

His head whipped around so he could regard her with his good eye. "Is that...?"

"A compliment, yes. Your accent. It's very... light. Barely there. You're easy to understand, unlike some of the other Irishmen here in town."

He visibly relaxed. "Oh, aye. Thank you," he replied.

They rode his silence until he negotiated the next turn. "This is very invigorating," Ella Mae said, glad she had tied the ribbons of her bonnet beneath her chin before she had left the store. Their speed seemed to create a wind that would have sent it flying off of her head otherwise.

He chuckled. "It is to drive as well." When they took the left corner onto Hill Street to head up to Prospect Street, he added, "Hold on."

Ella Mae didn't need to be told, and although it was frightening to think she could be tossed from the equipage at any moment, it was thrilling.

Would she be tossed off, though? For a moment, she imagined how John would casually snake an arm around her lower back to keep her seated. Her entire body seemed to shiver with excitement, which is probably why she couldn't help the giggle that escaped her lips when they turned onto Prospect Street. The horse was able to speed up once they were off the steep hill and onto more even terrain. "It's the second house up there on the left," she said, releasing her hold on her skirts to indicate the house.

"I know," he said. The horse trotted into the semicircular drive and came to a halt directly in front of the steps to the front door. "Stay put. I'll help you down," he said, before he stepped off the equipage and ambled around to her side.

"What do I do?" she asked, using one booted foot to feel for the top step as she clutched the pole. Once again, his hands were at her waist, and for a moment, she felt weightless as he lifted and lowered her until her feet touched the ground. She gripped his shoulders as a means to steady herself. "Thank you," she murmured, nearly breathless from the ride.

"Don't mention it. You're as light as a feather," he said, his hands still at her waist.

Ella Mae inhaled softly, finally lowering her hands from his shoulders. She was about to counter his claim but thought better of it. "So... you'll be at the ball?"

He nodded. "Will you save some dances for me?"

"I think you're allowed two," she murmured, her attention on his lips.

For a moment, she thought he might kiss her. Now

that the sun had set and twilight colored the sky, it was nearly dark. Who would see them?

Mrs. Jackson, probably.

Ella Mae's gaze darted to the the front of the house, where lights showed through the curtains of several windows. Mrs. Jackson would have dinner on the table soon.

"I intend to take what I'm allowed," he warned, moving to the back of the phaeton to retrieve her sewing basket from the rack.

She lifted a shoulder. "Then I shall look forward to it," she promised, taking the basket from him. A slight breeze brought with it the odor of autumn leaves and a reminder they were probably being watched.

He finally nodded. "Goodnight, Miss Montgomery." He gave a slight bow and bounded up onto the bench, oblivious to the cat who lounged in the back.

Ella Mae saw Sergeant, though, suppressing her scoff lest John misunderstand her annoyance with the mischievous cat. "Good night, Mr. O'Connor," she replied, dipping a curtsy. "And thank you for the ride. It was quite thrilling."

He lifted a hand to tip his cap as he gripped both reins in his other, and a moment later, the equipage was out of the drive and headed down the street.

The last she saw, Sergeant was still perched on the back of it.

Whatever does he think he's doing? she wondered.

CHAPTER 7
A TRYST CONTINUES

eanwhile, in a third story room at the DeSoto House Hotel

"Whatever *are* you doing over there?" Emma asked, sitting up from the bed where she had been dozing most of the afternoon. The remains of a rather large luncheon were scattered about the counterpane of the bed. The cat, Admiral, had disappeared beneath the bed some time ago, his "*yowl*" loud when Robert initiated their second round of lovemaking.

"Just ensuring our daughter makes it home all right," Robert said, pushing the drapes back into place before he moved to the side of the bed. He doffed the dressing gown he had put on at six o'clock, expecting he would have to wait some time before John O'Connor appeared below, driving a cart of some sort. Seeing a phaeton rather than a simple dog cart pull up in front of the hotel had surprised him. He was even more surprised when he spotted John escorting Ella Mae to it and then lifting her onto it. From his vantage, he couldn't tell if she was angry with the stablehand or if she appreciated his help.

If she was angry, he hoped she might forgive John O'Connor. The young man had been through enough in his life. Few in town knew what Robert knew—that John had left with the first group of young men to fight for the North in the war. That he had watched friends die before his eyes and then suffered a wound of his own when a gun misfired. Although the Army doctor had claimed he would never have use of his eye again, the local physician had other ideas. *Time is your friend, young man*, he had said, although he didn't make any promises.

"I meant to ask how our children were to get home today," Emma commented. "You've had my entire attention all day."

Robert grinned. "Then my evil plan has worked," he replied in a deep voice, attempting a guttural laugh that merely sounded comical.

His antics were answered with an odd howling sound.

"What was *that?*" Emma asked, pulling the bed covers up to her neck.

"Probably a ghost," he said, grinning at seeing how she cowered.

The howl sounded again, and he frowned. "Admiral, stop your yowling," he ordered. He disappeared from Emma's view for a moment, crouching on his hands and knees to peer under the bed.

A moment later, the large creature emerged from beneath a nearby chair, looking ever so proud of himself. "*Meow.*"

"You scared Emma half to death," he accused.

Admiral gave him what he surmised was an expression of offense before he rolled himself into a ball then stretched out on the floor. Robert could practically feel the vibrations from his purring through the floorboards.

"Yes, do make yourself comfortable," he murmured dryly.

Admiral narrowed his eyes before his head dropped to the floor.

Deciding he wasn't in the way, Robert rose from the floor and returned to the side of the bed. Removing the remains of their luncheon plate by plate, he regarded Emma with darkened eyes. "Now that we know most of the family is safe and sound…" He glanced back at the cat and arched a brow. Although Admiral opened his eyes and seemed intent on listening to his words, he didn't seem motivated to move. "…I do believe it's time I give you some more attention, my lady," Robert finished, doffing his robe before he climbed onto the bed.

Emma tittered. "I'll take all I can get."

It was nearly ten o'clock the following morning before they quietly checked out of the hotel. They took the back exit, where, thanks to prior arrangements having been made with John O'Connor, their curricle and horse were waiting.

CHAPTER 8
A LAWYER BRINGS NEWS

eanwhile, at the Galena Stable
Having completed hitching up four horses to a traveling coach parked behind the stable, John nodded to the driver. With a crack of a whip, the beasts surged into motion, and he returned to the dimly lit stable to resume his other duties.

The passing of Mr. Perkins the night before hadn't been a surprise. The news had reached him from the town's coroner, an elderly gentleman who had paid a visit to the stable shortly after John had returned from delivering Ella Mae Montgomery to her home. He had thanked the man for his information and went about completing his chores, his mind numb as he mucked a stall and refilled the huge water tank at the back of the stable.

The numbness wore off after a time, though, and

John had spent a restless night wondering about his future. Despite assurances he would have a position no matter what happened to Mr. Perkins, he couldn't help the sense of despair he felt at learning of the man's death.

What had been a surprise that morning was the visit from the man's lawyer. The dapper gentleman had appeared at the stable at precisely eight o'clock, a satchel clutched in one hand and a sheaf of papers in the other.

John had stiffened upon seeing Thomas Whitcomb, Esquire, sure he was there to relieve him of his duties. Probably give him his final pay and send him on his way, wherever that was to be.

Despite knowing Mr. Perkins' condition, John hadn't spent enough time considering options for his future. The work at the stable took so much of this time. When he wasn't concentrating on horses and equipage, he was thinking of Ella Mae Montgomery. Silently cursing his lot in life, he had been entirely unprepared for what the lawyer said.

"Mr. John O'Connor?"

"I am, sir." He had wiped his hands on a linen and was about to hold out his right hand when he realized the lawyer's hands were full. "What can I do for you?"

"It's what I'm here to do for *you*, young man. If you'll sign these papers, you'll find you're the new owner of Galena Stable, horses and all," Mr. Whitcomb announced. "Do you… do you have an office where we can talk, perhaps?" he asked, glancing about.

"Of a sort," John replied, staring at the lawyer in

disbelief. "Uh… this way," he said, leading them to a room filled with tack, saddles, brushes, and a counter where he took payment for services rendered.

"From your reaction, I take it Mr. Perkins didn't warn you he had included you in his last will and testament?" Mr. Whitcomb asked. He set the papers on the counter.

John shook his head. "He did not." After the shock had worn off some, he dipped his head. "Which has me wondering if I'm inheriting some debts to go along with the business?" he guessed, wincing at hearing how ungrateful he sounded.

"No debts, other than what you might incur from here on out," Mr. Whitcomb assured him. "Apparently you're already familiar with the vendors? Your sources for hay and such?"

"I am, sir," John acknowledged.

The lawyer pulled out a quill pen and nodded to the ink pot sitting at one end of the counter. "I just need your signature here… and here," he said, pointing to several lines on a paper filled with perfectly printed words. "Here's your copy of the deed for the property… and your copy of the transfer of ownership," Mr. Whitcomb said, handing over several pages once John had finished signing his name and the ink had dried.

John stared in awe as he was given the documentation proving he was the new owner of Galena Stable. "All the carriages, too?" he asked in a whisper.

Mr. Whitcomb chucked. "All of it, Mr. O'Connor. Should you ever need my services, here's my card."

John thanked the lawyer and shook his hand. Grinned when Mr. Whitcomb congratulated him. Frowned when he realized he was responsible for not only the horses he now owned, but also for the building in which they resided along with all manner of equipage in various states of repair—and disrepair.

"I'm a business owner," he murmured, once the lawyer had taken his leave of the stable.

There hadn't been time to celebrate. There hadn't even been time for a drink at the nearby saloon. There had been horses to hitch and stalls to muck, and water troughs and grain buckets to refill. He didn't even want to announce his new status to the world let alone the citizens of Galena. There was only one person he wanted to tell, and he wasn't even sure how she would react.

Would Ella Mae Montgomery care that he was now the proprietor of Galena Stable?

Well, there was only one way to find out.

The masquerade ball was the next evening. He could probably afford a few pieces of clothing—a black shirt, black trousers, and a black mantle—items he could wear for other occasions beside the ball. He already owned a pair of boots, although they had seen better days. A short top hat would serve him well, too.

When business slowed later in the afternoon, he took what he needed from the till and headed down Main Street to a men's clothing store.

An hour later, he emerged with a paper-wrapped bundle of clothing, a black bandana, and a new hat.

He could hardly wait for Ella Mae to see him at the ball.

CHAPTER 9
A MOTHER AND DAUGHTER TALK

The following evening Emma tightened the strings of Ella Mae's corset before tying the ends into a bow. "You never did show me your costume," she said, stepping to the side to help with lifting a crinoline into place around her daughter's waist. She tied the strings of the waistband and helped Ella Mae to pull on a petticoat.

"That's because I finished it only moments ago," Ella Mae replied, regarding her reflection in the cheval mirror with a critical eye. "I haven't even seen it on me."

"Then we'll both be surprised," Emma said, moving to the bed to gather up the white gown. "This fabric is gorgeous. Why, this could be a wedding gown," she remarked, studying the tiny stitches making up the seams and the white flowers embroidered along the neckline. "You do such beautiful work, young lady. Your talents with a needle far surpass those of Mrs. Watkins."

Ella Mae grinned. "She was an excellent teacher," she claimed, bending down while her mother held the skirt so she could pull it over her head. After a good deal of wriggling, shifting, and draping, the full skirt finally settled over the petticoat and crinoline. Reaching for the separate bodice, Emma held it open so Ella Mae could push her arms into the sleeves. "Hold still, and I'll do up the buttons," she offered.

"Of course," Ella Mae replied, unaware General had snuck out from beneath the bed and was hiding under the crinoline. "You never said what you did during your trip to Dubuque." From the moment her parents had returned home the noon before, she could tell they had enjoyed their time together. Her mother's color had been high during dinner, and she had caught her father staring at her when his attention was usually on his food.

Emma tittered. "Truth be told, I didn't see anything of Dubuque. I only had eyes for your father," she claimed.

Ella Mae turned her head so her chin rested on her shoulder. "I could say the same about him for you during dinner this evening. Whatever did you do to that poor man?" she asked, grinning. "He's positively in love with you."

"He is indeed. And I am in love with him, even after all these years," Emma admitted. She finished the last button and moved to stand in front of her daughter. "I do hope that sooner rather than later, you, too, will love a man as much as I love him," she whispered.

Ella Mae dipped her head. "What if... what if I already like someone enough to think that I might love him someday?"

Emma's eyes rounded. "Do you? Like someone, I mean?"

Lifting a shoulder, Ella Mae hesitated to respond. "Oh, I do, I suppose. We have known one another practically our entire lives, but it's only been lately that I think he could be more than an acquaintance. More than a friend."

"Then... what has you so concerned?"

Ella Mae sighed. "I fear he may not be good enough in Father's eyes," she whispered. "He's not wealthy."

"Neither was your father." Wincing at hearing her words aloud, Emma sat on the edge of the bed and allowed a long sigh. "I know you will want him to approve, but you will have to follow your heart first and foremost."

"Did you? Follow your heart. Mother?"

Emma stared at her daughter for a few moments, her gaze on her mind's eye. "I don't think I was completely in love with him that first day, but... I think I was by the end of the second."

"Mother," Ella Mae scolded. "He loved you from the start. Or so he claims."

Tittering, Emma blushed. "So he claims," she repeated, arching a brow. "You can be sure we were thoroughly in love with one another when we married," she stated.

Ella Mae regarded her reflection in the cheval mirror. "This does look as if it would make the perfect wedding gown," she murmured.

"Well, if not a bride, then who… or *what* exactly… are you going to be this evening?" her mother asked, rising from the bed to admire the gown. The white-on-white roses woven into the surface of the fabric appeared to shimmer like satin, while the background looked to be silk.

Ella Mae turned to face her bureau and pulled a flat package from the top. "An angel,," she replied. "These are my wings, and there's a halo here, too. Father ordered them for me." She unwrapped a set of small wired wings, unfolding them before allowing their attached lengths of ribbon to dangle from where they were joined in the middle. Rows of goose feathers had been stitched to the satin fabric made stiff by the wire inserts.

Emma inhaled softly. "I'm quite jealous," she murmured. "The gown for my come-out wasn't nearly this nice," she claimed, taking the wings from her daughter and placing them at her back. She threaded the ribbons around the tops of Ella Mae's shoulders and then under her arms, tying the ends together at her back before hiding the knot behind the wings. "Can you move your arms?"

Ella Mae held them up and out, pantomiming how she would hold them during a dance. "They work," she said happily.

"They had better. They cost enough," her father said

from the doorway. Despite his comment, he was grinning as he leaned against the jamb, his arms crossed over attire similar to what a member of the landed gentry might have worn when the country was founded. His gaze swept over her and then went to his wife, who was dressed in a royal blue gown from the prior century, her hair mostly covered with a white mobcap. "There should be a halo with those wings," he added.

Emma unwrapped tissue from around a yellow painted halo. Attached to it was a wire that protruded from a headband adorned with hair combs. She studied the flattened ornament before realizing she needed to bend the head support so the halo would appear to hover over its wearer's head. She inserted the combs into Ella Mae's coiffure and then stepped back to regard her daughter with a sad expression. "My little angel," she murmured, tears pricking the corners of her eyes.

"Mother," Ella Mae scolded, at the same moment Bobby appeared next to his father.

"Ugh. I'm so glad I don't have to go," he announced, his face screwed into a grimace.

"Just you wait, young man," Emma warned. "A few years from now, you'll be dressing like a dandy so you can dance with Sarah Watkins."

"Eww," he replied, his eyes wide with horror. He disappeared into his bedchamber as his parents chuckled.

"The curricle is ready. Let's be on our way," Robert said, offering his arm to his wife. She took it, and the three of them made their way down the steps and to the equipage.

No one noticed that both General and Admiral had joined them in the curricle.

CHAPTER 10
PREPARING FOR A BALL

A half-hour later

Despite his having inherited everything in the three rooms he occupied above the stable, John was still hesitant to help himself to the nicer items he had discovered during the past few months he had worked there. At first, he was uncomfortable rifling through the trunks and boxes stacked in one corner of the room in which he slept. These had been another man's possessions, possibly someone other than Mr. Perkins.

In a valet's box, meant to hold cuff links and buckles, he found a cravat pin that appeared to be topped with a diamond. He was sure it was merely paste until he stabbed it into the mail coach knot of his neck cloth and admired how it winked in the light from a nearby hurricane lamp. What if it was real?

Tucked into the black velvet at the very bottom, he discovered a gold ring. He slid it onto his pinkie and held out his hand, sure it was real gold. Would it fit one of Ella Mae's fingers? If so, perhaps his poor excuse for a betrothal ring, one he'd had the blacksmith fashion earlier that morning, wouldn't be needed.

He once again pondered what he planned to do that evening. Without encouragement from Robert Montgomery and Mr. Perkins' death, John never would have considered taking a wife—at least not at his age. But his circumstances had changed, and he feared if he waited too long to secure a promise of marriage from Ella Mae, she might end up married to someone else.

Thoughts of marriage reminded him he needed to make it to the masquerade ball.

He found a pair of riding boots, black and shined to a high gloss, tucked behind an empty trunk. The boots fit fine once he pulled on another pair of stockings. As to whether or not he would be able to dance in them, he wouldn't find out until later that night.

Dressed in black from head to toe, John wondered if he might have been considered fashionable back East attending a night at the theatre. Not interested in appearing fashionable at the masquerade ball—he wanted to look like a highwayman—he tied a black bandana around his head so it covered his nose and lower face. With his eye patch covering his injured eye, his other eye required a similar patch but with an opening in the middle so he could see.

He fashioned the mask from a strip of black felt he had found in an old sewing basket and tied it behind his head. Regarding his reflection in a small shaving mirror, he realized he would not wish to meet himself in a dark alley. He appeared every bit the highwayman. Adding the top hat didn't lessen the effect but rather made him seem more respectable.

Remembering Ella Mae's costume would be white—at least what he could see of the gown she had been sewing when he had shopped in the dry goods store two days ago–John wondered if the contrast would be too much. Dressed in white, she would look like an angel while he would look like the Devil incarnate.

Too late now, he thought as he made his way out of his rooms above the stable and down the stairs. Grabbing a black riding crop from the tack room before he locked the stable doors, he headed for the DeSoto House Hotel.

Up and down the boardwalk, other townsfolk were making their way toward the hotel dressed in all manner of costumes. On a normal day, he would have felt too self-conscious to be seen in public in Galena. The son of a poor laborer, wearing an eye patch? Tonight, he felt empowered. In the ballroom on the fourth floor of the DeSoto House Hotel, no one would know his identity, at least not right away.

Ella Mae would, though. They had discussed this particular disguise. She owed him two dances, but most importantly, he hoped she might be willing to commit to more. Far more.

CHAPTER 11
THE MASQUERADE BALL

A few minutes later, at the DeSoto House Hotel

The faint music from a five-piece chamber orchestra reached Ella Mae's ears before she and her parents topped the stairs leading to the fourth floor of the hotel. Inside the ballroom, the fully-lit chandeliers were reflected in the silvered glass panels between the room's velvet-draped windows, enhancing a golden glow that warmed the complexions of everyone who stepped inside. Murmurs and titters of laughter could be heard as guests arrived dressed in a variety of costumes and disguises.

That is, until *he* arrived.

A collective gasp sounded when a black-clad man entered the ballroom, his menacing appearance made more so in that his face was almost entirely covered in black. The mantle he wore, opened at the front, revealed a shirt, cravat, waistcoat, trousers, and boots—all in black. Even the hair showing beneath his black top hat was black. In one black-gloved hand, he carried a riding crop.

"Who is he?" Emma whispered, her arm on her husband's as they took a turn about the room. On the other side of her, Ella Mae said, "*That* is Mr. O'Connor."

Robert chuckled softly as his wife inhaled sharply. "No. It cannot be," Emma said in awe. "Why, is he wearing a diamond in his cravat?"

"I rather doubt that," Ella Mae whispered. "It's probably paste."

For a moment it was so quiet, Ella Mae was sure she could hear a pin drop on the varnished wood floor. That was the moment General chose to peek out from beneath her skirt to let out a mournful *yowl.*

A woman off to the left, dressed a gaudy saloon girl costume, gasped loudly. "The ghost!' she cried out in fright.

As if on cue, General loudly *meowed,* which had those nearest to Ella Mae giggling as they pointed to the calico.

"General!" Emma scolded. The cat immediately disappeared beneath Ella Mae's gown.

"Fear not, my angel, I will see to the brigand," John said in a deep voice, rushing to stand before Ella Mae. He bowed deeply, holding onto one edge of his mantle with his free hand as he did so. The dramatic bow had several people clapping and a few laughing before another round of costumed ball-goers arrived to take the attention from him and Ella Mae.

"Clever costume, Mr. O'Connor," Robert remarked. "And it would be rather fashionable if you were to replace the shirt with a white one. Why, you would be set for an evening in St. Louis."

"Or a wedding," Ella Mae murmured, her eyes rounding when she realized she had said the words out loud.

"Thank you, Mr. Montgomery, Miss Montgomery. I'll be sure to remember that," John replied.

That was the moment the orchestra began the dancing music. Several couples, including her parents, moved to the center of the room, the ladies curtsying to the gentlemen's bows before beginning their set.

"You look like an angel," John murmured, leaning close so his words wouldn't be heard by anyone but Ella Mae.

She inhaled softly and turned to discover he was standing rather close to her. "And you are perfection as a highwayman," she enthused. "Not that I've ever actually seen one. However did you put together your costume so quickly?"

John lifted a shoulder. "Had some help from a clerk at Mr. Watkins' shop," he replied, referring to the ready-made menswear store. "Are you enjoying your come-out?"

She regarded him with a smirk. "I would if I had someone with whom to dance."

"Will you dance with me?"

"Of course," she replied, reaching up to place her hand on his shoulder as he took her other hand in his. They stutter-stepped a few times before they were in sync with one another, which made conversation difficult.

"I understand condolences are in order," she said, once they had merged into the circle of other dancers. "It's a shame about Mr. Perkins. Father told us about him during dinner this evening."

"Thank you," he replied. "I've known him... *knew* him a long time, and he always said I would have a position should I need one. He kept his word," he explained.

Ella Mae seemed to hesitate before she asked, "Where did you go?"

He blinked, his visible brow furrowing so it nearly disappeared behind his mask. "What do you mean?"

"After we finished school. Why didn't I see you about town?"

Hesitating a moment, and not only because he had to steer them around another couple, John seemed to think on his response before he finally said, "I went off to war."

Ella Mae's eyes widened. "You fought for the Union?"

He nodded. "I did. Until my eye sustained a hit from a misfire, and then I was discharged. Honorably, at least, but..." He shrugged. "Not how I expected it to go."

Wincing, Ella Mae had to resist the urge to ask what

he had expected. She instead asked, "What will you do now that Mr. Perkins has died? Will the new owner keep you on at the stable, do you suppose?"

Grinning behind the bandana, John said, "I had a long talk with him yesterday, in fact. I not only get to keep my position, he has put me in charge of the entire operation."

"Really?" Her eyes rounded with joy. "Why, that's wonderful. I mean..." She paused when the dance required a more intricate move. "That is, if *you* think it is."

He chuckled. "I do, actually. I am the new owner, Ella Mae. The stable, the horses, the equipage, the property... I have the deed to all of it," he stated, apparently unaware he had used her given name.

"*You're* the new owner of Galena Stable?" she asked in awe, her query sounding at exactly the same moment the music ended. The dancers nearest them turned with looks of curiosity and surprise, and General once again took the opportunity to make an appearance and *yowl* from the edge of her hem.

"The ghost is back," an older gentleman called out from where he was seated with three others, engaged in a game of cards. His comment was met with a round of laughter and gasps from those who hadn't been in the ballroom before the dance had started.

Grinning, John said, "That reminds me," as he led her to the refreshment table. "Sergeant was riding on the back of the phaeton the night I drove you home," he said. "I didn't discover him until I was on my way up to my rooms above the stable." He offered her a glass of punch.

"Oh, I'm so sorry," she replied, sure her face was bright red, and not from the exertions of the dance.

"No need to be. I feared you would miss him, though."

"Hardly," she replied, arching a blonde brow.

A loud, low *howl* sounded from the other side of the ballroom. The music hadn't yet started for the next dance, so conversations suddenly ceased. Sure General was to blame, Ella Mae glanced down to discover him peeking out from beneath her gown. "That wasn't you," she said, her gaze darting about to see others in the ballroom had grown nervous. When the howling happened again, this time longer and louder, an older woman screamed.

"That was the real ghost!" someone else called out.

Several women rushed for the doors while some of the gentlemen pulled their wives closer to their sides.

That's when Ella Mae saw him.

Admiral.

The cat's head was poking out from beneath her mother's costume, the orange fur a stark contrast to the blue skirts of her Georgian-era gown.

"Admiral," she scolded, loud enough to be heard across the room.

The orchestra chose that moment to begin the next dance set, the music drowning out some of the sounds of pandemonium as a few were still trying to escape the ballroom while others were laughing at the cat.

"This is positively mortifying," Ella Mae complained. "On the night of my come-out, no less."

"Paawsitively?" John repeated, his visible eye conveying his humor at hearing her comment.

She scoffed. "There was no pun intended, I assure you. He's become such a pest. *All* of them have become pests." Across the room, her father had scooped up Admiral and was headed for the door. Apparently deciding he didn't wish to be bodily removed from the ballroom, General darted out from beneath her skirt and followed her father.

Next to her, John chuckled. "If it's any consolation, they have certainly provided a good deal of entertainment this evening."

"It's not," she mewled. After a moment, a grin lifted the edge of her lips. "They have managed to make it less crowded in here, though," she added, arching a brow.

"More room for us to dance," he said, holding out his hand.

She glanced up at him. "This will be our second. You're only allowed two," she reminded him.

He seemed entirely too pleased with himself. "Not according to your father."

Her eyes widened in delight. "Why John O'Connor, whatever did you say to him?"

John was already pulling her into his arms for the

dance. "That would be between him and me," he responded.

Stunned to learn she had been a topic of conversation, Ella Mae blushed. "Whatever did he say to you?" she pressed.

Several steps into the dance, John leaned down and whispered in her ear. "I'll tell you later."

Scoffing at hearing his reply, Ella Mae gave him a quelling glance. "You had better," she said.

For the next few sets, she danced with others, including her father. He left her standing in front of John, though, and they spent most of the next dance simply staring at one another.

That is, until John said, "Marry me, Ella Mae."

CHAPTER 12
A PROPOSAL

*E*lla Mae stared at John, her mouth dropping open when she realized he had removed the bandana from his face before he put voice to his proposal.

"Did my father…?" She paused, her eyes widening in wonder. "Oh, John," she breathed, her gaze darting about in search of her parents. She found them standing in a corner, watching her as if they, too, were waiting for her response. "Are you quite sure?"

John gave a start. "Ella Mae Montgomery, I haven't been so sure about anything in my entire life," he replied. "I would have asked before I left, but—"

"Yes. Yes, I will marry you," she said, grinning in delight. "I cannot believe this is happening on the night of my come-out."

He grinned, the dimple appearing at the base of his cheek. "Until Mr. Whitcomb paid me a visit to inform me of my… inheritance, I didn't think I could ask you," he explained. "At least, not yet. But as the new owner of Galena Stable, I think I can afford to keep you in a manner to which you've—"

"I don't require the same accommodations as my mother," she interrupted. "Not that my father had to be the one to provide them."

John furrowed his brows. "I plan to spoil you, Ella Mae."

She grinned, stood on tiptoes, and gave him a quick peck on his cheek. "I might allow it," she said, grinning in delight. "Oh, if only we could wed tonight," she breathed. "We have witnesses, and my parents are here," she added, gazing up at him as tears collected in the corners of her eyes. "We're both dressed in such elegant finery."

John stared down at her, finally blinking twice before he glanced about the ballroom. "There must be a minister around here somewhere," he murmured. "You are certainly dressed for a wedding." He held out one of his hands. "I have a ring I can give you." He pulled it from his pinkie.

Ella Mae giggled before her eyes widened at seeing the Presbyterian minister approaching them from near to where her parents were standing. "Hello, Reverend Jenkins," she said.

"This is rather… *unusual,* but I suppose we can see to the formalities in a day or two," the minister said as he pulled a small book from his pocket. He nodded to where her parents stood. "Your father has already given permission for you to wed, I take it?" he asked.

"He has," John stated.

Ella Mae inhaled softly. "He has?"

"I have," Robert affirmed. He and her mother had joined them to stand before the minister.

Removing her lace mask, Ella Mae handed it to her mother while John removed the one from his good eye. The two turned to face the minister. Behind him, those left in the ballroom, wearing costumes and watching in wonder, paid witness to their wedding.

When Reverend Jenkins' asked if anyone objected to the union, there was silence. Not even a *meow* met his query, so the man proceeded with reciting the marriage rites in a simple ceremony.

With a murmured "With this ring I wed thee" and a pair of "I will"s, the minister's declaration that they were man and wife had most in the ballroom applauding.

Meows could be heard from somewhere outside the ballroom, which had most laughing but her mother grimacing in dismay.

"Champagne for all," Robert Montgomery called out. The room erupted in shouts of joy.

For the next hour, the orchestra continued to play, and except for the next dance, which Ella Mae spent with her father, John claimed all the rest of the dances until the clock struck midnight.

Emma approached Ella Mae when it was apparent the last dance of the evening was about to begin. Tears pricked the corners of her eyes. "There's nothing else I can tell you that I haven't already said," she whispered. "Trust him. Your father certainly does," she added before she pulled her daughter into an embrace. "I'll pay a call on you in a day or two, Mrs. O'Connor."

Ella Mae gasped softly. "Mother," she breathed. Before she could say more, Emma and Robert were headed for the exit.

A moment later, a distant howling had the rest of the ball goers rushing for the exit. John and Ella Mae grinned and watched until everyone else had departed before they made their way down the stairs and to the front desk of the hotel.

"You room is ready, Mr. O'Connor," the clerk stated, handing him a key. "Your luggage has already been delivered."

Ella Mae glanced up at him in surprise. "Luggage?" she repeated, sure her new husband was blushing.

"I might have made some arrangements in advance," he hedged, offering his arm. "With your father, and the reverend, and the hotel," he added.

Inhaling softly, Ella Mae stared at him. "What if I hadn't agreed to wed you this evening?"

He chuckled softly and lifted a shoulder. "I would have courted you until you did agree," he stated.

Grinning, she placed a hand on his arm. "Well, then, lead the way, Mr. O'Connor."

His humor still apparent, John escorted her up the stairs.

"Where will we live?" she asked, once they had reached the first floor landing.

He dipped his head. "I have rooms above the stable," he replied. "But I'll be in search of a house for us as soon as I can."

"Our own house. So soon?"

He angled his head to one side. "I promised I would spoil you," he reminded her. "And I intend to start this evening."

Ella Mae suppressed a giggle. "Mr. O'Connor—"

"Call me John." He paused before one of the doors and inserted the key into the lock. A *snick* sounded before the door opened to reveal a room lined in flowered wallpaper and furnished with a bed, an upholstered chair , an escritoire, and a bench.

"Call me Ella Mae," she countered. She inhaled softly. "You're quite a conniving young man, aren't you?" she added, her gaze sweeping the room.

"My mother used to say that to my father." He arched a dark brow. "When you say it, it doesn't make me sound so bad, though."

Her eyes rounded. "Whatever do you mean?"

"Your hint of an accent. The way you say your words, all proper like, but not snooty. You could call me a bastard and I wouldn't mind."

She inhaled softly. "I would never call you that, John."

"You might after what I'm about to do to you." His warning was barely audible.

Ella Mae's eyes rounded when he bent down and touched his lips to hers. She didn't back away, though—not that she could since she was pressed against the door—and instead she parted her lips in invitation.

Before she knew it, his lips captured hers. She gripped the fabric of his sleeves with both hands in an effort to stay upright.

She tasted the punch and the champagne he had drunk. Her knees felt as if they had turned to jelly, and not just from the champagne she had imbibed.

When he pulled away, she let out a mewl of protest. He grinned. "I think one of us might be feeling a bit drunk," he whispered.

"Oh," she replied, disappointment evident in her response. "Does that mean you wouldn't have kissed me if you were sober?"

"*I'm* not the one who's feeling the champagne," he countered, his brow once again arching as a grin appeared.

"It was excellent champagne," she whispered, a moment before she stood on tiptoes and kissed him. Her hands reached up to his shoulders as she pressed against him. She moaned when his tongue invaded her mouth and slid across her teeth.

She had never been kissed before, but she wanted it to go on and on. Wanted him to hold her closer, and then was sure he could read her mind, for his hand had moved to the small of her back and he was pulling her hard against him.

When he relaxed his hold on her, she stared up at him, her eyes finally focusing on his one good eye. "I've actually never kissed a man before."

John regarded his new wife with a look of relief. "Well I should hope not."

Grinning, Ella Mae reached up and gave him a quick kiss on the lips. "I think I shall enjoy being married to you."

~

"Then I am even more blessed than I thought I was yesterday morning," John replied, referring to the way he had felt the moment he learned he had inherited the stable.

Ella Mae gave him a brilliant smile. "I am so pleased you think so."

He angled his head to one side. Holding her like this —her shoulders wrapped in his arms and their bodies pressed close—did have him feeling rather blessed.

Blessed and regretful, for what sort of life might they have had if he had never gone off to war?

John gave his head a shake. He hadn't been looking for someone back then. Hadn't been of a mind to share a hardscrabble life in a burgeoning town. The responsibility of seeing to it his father had meals and made it to work every morning was quite enough in his teens. Then, given the timing of his father's death, it only made sense to leave Galena with the band of volunteers

Colonel Grant had hastily assembled. He never imagined that in less than a year's time, he would survive military training, travel over five-hundred miles, and fight in several bloody battles only to lose an eye and be discharged.

So why had Robert Montgomery decided *he* was the one who should marry his daughter?

Perhaps he had known of Mr. Perkins' plan to bequeath the stable to him. Perhaps Ella Mae had mentioned she knew him from school.

John knew it wasn't out of pity, but perhaps the man had seen something of himself in him. Saw an opportunity to be a matchmaker.

He glanced down to discover a cat staring up at him. He had to suppress the urge to chuckle.

"What do you find so amusing?" Ella Mae asked, pulling him from his reverie.

"I blame it all on the cats," he stated.

"*Credit* them, don't you mean?" she countered, finding both Sergeant and Colonel were watching them with great interest. Where they had come from, she had no idea.

"Now you've gone and done it," he said as he lowered his forehead to hers.

"What have I done?"

"Whatever it is *they* want you to do."

"Which is... what?"

John glanced back at Colonel and arched a brow. "Well?"

"*Meow*." Colonel replied, as if he was providing some sort of answer.

Sergeant joined Colonel, the two posed in identical sitting positions and looking every bit the twins they were. They gazed up at John and Ella Mae for a moment before they settled onto their sides.

"See?" John said, turning to discover Ella Mae staring at him rather than at the cats. Beneath his hold, something shifted in her.

"Does that mean they will allow us to make love this evening?" Ella Mae asked, her voice quiet.

John's brows drew together, his good humor gone in an instant. "Mrs. O'Connor—"

"Ella Mae. You can call me Ella Mae." She seemed to give her comment a second thought. "Although I do like being called Mrs. O'Connor."

"Ella Mae, I have no intention of allowing you out of my sight for at least the next ten hours. They won't, either."

She blinked up at him. "That long?"

"We have the room until noon. That is, if we don't have to be somewhere else."

"I don't," she claimed.

He paused. "Would you like to go to bed?" he asked, his voice sounding breathy.

Her gaze darted toward the bed. "Will you be in it?"

It was John's turn to blink. "If you'll allow it."

"Well, shouldn't I insist on it?" She glanced over at

the cats, and this time Colonel responded with a rather loud, "*Meow*."

John scoffed softly. "Just how much champagne did you drink?"

"I didn't even finish my third glass. I feared I might be unable to walk if I drank any more than that."

He chuckled as he lifted the halo from her coiffure. "Do you know what happens on a wedding night?"

She nodded. "Indeed. In fact, I've been spending the past few afternoons imagining what it would be like to make love to you."

Astonished at hearing her words, John chuckled. "Oh, well this should go well," he said with relief. "You'll show me how then?"

Not sure if he was teasing her nor not, Emma glanced up to discover his eye had darkened until it was nearly black.

"Something tells me I won't have to," she whispered.

"Something tells me I won't be opening the stable until the afternoon," he whispered, before leading her to the bed.

Glancing at the two cats who watched from the other side of the room, Emma gave them a wink as John undid the buttons at her back.

CHAPTER 13
A WEDDING NIGHT

a few minutes later

John lit the only hurricane lamp in the room and worried Ella Mae had changed her mind when she stood by the side of the bed and audibly sighed. Earlier that day, he had made a deal with the hotel owner. In exchange for the use of the room for his wedding night, he would board the owner's horse for a month.

Judging from the fine linens, two feather pillows, and the counterpane on top of the bed, he decided he had the better part of the deal.

"I take it you've changed your mind?"

Ella Mae shook her head. "Oh, I haven't changed my mind. I am hoping the bed doesn't break, is all." She turned and reached out to pluck the cravat pin from his neckcloth.

Despite the seriousness of her words, John couldn't

help but laugh. "Goodness, Ella Mae, what are you planning to do to me?" He sobered when he noticed how she stared at the diamond tip. "It's probably just paste," he murmured.

"I don't think it is," she said in awe. "Where ever did you get it?"

He shrugged. "It came with my inheritance," he said. "Along with everything else in the stable." He took it from her and placed it on the small desk.

She undid the knot of his cravat. "I believe Mr. Perkins must have thought of you as the son he never had," she said, unwinding the black silk from around his neck.

"I think you might be right," he agreed, dropping a kiss on her forehead.

She undid the button at the top of his collarless shirt, and watched him grin when she pulled up on his shirt tails until they were free of his trousers.

He divested himself of the garment in one quick move then once again sobered when he saw her look of uncertainty.

Or perhaps it was awe.

"You haven't seen a man without his shirt on, have you?"

"Only in drawings," she admitted. "Mostly of Greek Gods. Oh, and a few lead miners." She took in the crisp curls dusting his chest. His nipples were erect, much like hers were. Despite the soft fabric of her chemise under her corset, they felt as if they were chafed.

He stepped behind her. "I hope I don't disappoint," he said in a whisper, undoing the row of buttons at her back and the one holding her skirt closed at the top. Beneath it, he discovered ties for her petticoat and crinoline and began undoing them.

Ella Mae tittered softly. "Hardly." She took a deep breath at the same moment her skirts and petticoats dropped to the floor in a round puddle. She lowered the bodice from her arms and tossed it onto the nearby chair. Left wearing only a corset over a chemise and her stockings, she suddenly felt vulnerable. "I hope I don't disappoint you."

"I rather doubt that would be possible." He moved to stand in front of her and glanced down at her shapely limbs. The thin chemise ended well above her knees and did nothing to hide the dark triangle at the apex of her thighs.

She stepped out of the huge ring of fabric. "I am left wondering what it was I did that left you with such a good opinion of me."

A smirk lifted the corners of his lips. "I shared a schoolroom with you for... for ten years," he claimed. "You were the nicest of all the girls. And the prettiest," he claimed as he regarded her corset. He reached out and encouraged her to turn around with his hands at her waist.

"You never... courted another woman?" Her eyes suddenly rounded. "While you were in the army? I hear there are women—"

"Camp followers," he stated, leaning forward to place a kiss on the side of her head. "And no, I didn't."

He undid the ties of her corset. "Am I doing this right?" he asked when he finally had the bow undone at the bottom.

"I cannot imagine how you could do it wrong." Even through the stiff fabric of her corset, she felt the warmth of his hands, and the careful way he barely touched her as he struggled with loosening the ties. "When you left town... did you leave someone behind?"

"I did not," he replied. "Can't leave anyone behind if I didn't have someone," he added.

"Not even a..." She swallowed. "A lady of the evening?"

"Not even." He clamped his mouth shut, surprised she would mention the prostitutes that serviced the miners.

She turned to look up at him. "Would you tell me... why not?"

He shrugged. "None of them were you," he murmured.

She stared at him for several seconds, her breath held. "Oh, John," she finally said on a sigh, wrapping an arm around his neck while she stood on tiptoes to kiss him. When she ended the kiss, she placed a hand over his, guiding it so it cupped one of her breasts as she pushed the corset from her body.

Although it didn't provide enough light for the entire room, the hurricane lamp was close enough to illuminate her. Ella Mae felt far too exposed, but then she saw how the light played off John's chest, and she inhaled softly. "You're so... broad," she whispered.

"Is that bad?" He rubbed a thumb over one of her nipples, the nubbin leaving a silhouette in the fabric of her chemise.

She inhaled sharply, which had her breast filling his hand. He repeated the move on her other nipple, and she mewled softly. "No," she managed. She placed the pads of her fingers against his warm skin, trailing them through dark curls and down his stomach to the top of his trousers. She knew what caused the bulge below that, even if she hadn't seen one directly. Cupping her hand along its length, she gently pressed it.

John inhaled sharply and covered her hand with one of his. "Careful," he whispered hoarsely.

She pulled her hand away. "Did I hurt you?"

"Exactly the opposite." He fumbled with the buttons of his trousers.

Ella Mae understood his struggle and immediately went to work undoing the fastenings. The trousers opened, and his manhood sprang out as she pushed the garment down his hips. "Oh, my," she whispered.

"Is that a good 'oh my' or an 'oh my' of disappointment?" He sat on the edge of the bed and pulled his boots and stockings from his feet, placing the footwear at the end of the bed.

Ella Mae gave a one-shouldered shrug. "Mayhap of fright?" She took in his nakedness from head to toe and back to his crotch when he stood and pulled her into his arms. She resettled her cheek against his warm skin. One of his arms had wrapped behind her shoulders while the other was at the back of her waist, as if he feared she might try to leave the room. She glanced up at him. "You're very warm."

"There is a reason," he remarked dryly.

She pulled one of her hands from behind his back and smoothed it between them until it came in contact with his manhood. Drawing a finger down the side of it, she paused when his breathing hitched.

"It's so soft," she murmured.

"I beg your pardon?"

She blinked and then drew the finger up the vein that throbbed along its length. "The skin. It's like velvet." She added her thumb and gently squeezed, her hold on him giving way when he pulled back. "Like velvet stretched over a metal rod."

"I don't think it's ever been this hard." He took her hand and guided her fingers to wrap around the shaft and then moved them up and down, his breaths shortening when she tightened her hold. "I fear if you do that much longer, I'll come too quick."

"Won't you feel pleasure? From your... your release?" A bead of moisture had formed at the tip of his manhood. She drew her thumb over it, spreading it out as John inhaled sharply.

"How do you know about that?" he asked between gasps for air.

Ella Mae glanced up at him. "Mother says making love is really quite pleasurable."

He nodded before he remembered she hadn't experienced the intense pleasure of sexual congress. "I think we're about to find out."

"Will you...?"

She couldn't finish the sentence when he suddenly pulled the chemise from her body and scooped her into his arms. He had her in the middle of the bed and his body atop hers before she could react. His mouth covered one of her breasts, his tongue flicking across her nipple until she whimpered. Moving to the other side, he murmured something about how beautiful she was before doing the same with her other breast.

Needing something to hold onto, Ella Mae speared her fingers into his black hair, her fingernails scraping his scalp. She felt him shiver, heard his labored breathing, and thrilled when one of his hands smoothed down her belly, through her damp curls, and to her thighs. Knowing some of what to do, she parted her knees in invitation and almost drew them shut when his fingers slid past her folds and circled her most private place.

"Did I hurt you?" He stilled his fingers.

"You startled me, is all. Do go on. Please."

He chuckled softly, reveling in how she angled her hips to welcome his touch. When he heard her breaths shorten and her soft whimpers increase in volume, he quickened his ministrations until he heard his name called out and her body quivered. He ceased moving his hand when one of hers suddenly covered it.

His need for her too great, he didn't give her time to catch her breath. He hooked his arms beneath her knees to lift them and then pushed his manhood into her in a tentative thrust.

Ella Mae's back arched in response, and he seemed to drive deeper into her before he pulled nearly all the way out of her.

He might have paused to prevent what he feared was about to happen, but his body required surcease. He had been too close to his release the moment before he lifted her onto the bed. Now that her thighs gripped his and her fingernails were leaving half-moon indentations in his back, John knew she was his. Only a few more thrusts, and his entire body spasmed, the intense pleasure blinding him to everything but the soft body beneath him.

He managed to hold himself up on his outstretched arms. Dipping his head down, he kissed Ella Mae until he no longer had any strength. He collapsed atop her, his head ending face down in the pillow next to hers.

"Are you all right?" she asked in a whisper.

He chuckled and eventually lifted himself onto his elbows. Glancing down, he saw how her breasts mounded against his chest. "My angel. You are so beautiful." He was about to roll off of her when she tightened her grip on his back.

"Where do you think you're going?"

He dropped his head to her shoulder. "Next to you, if that's all right."

"You're still... inside me," she murmured.

Grinning, he nodded. "My angel, trust me when I tell you it's absolute heaven."

"Then don't leave me."

John kissed her on the lips. "Um.. well... " He glanced to his left and then to the right before saying, "Hold on to me."

"I thought I..." Ella Mae let out a squeak when he suddenly rolled onto his back, taking her body with him. One of her knees ended up so close to the edge of the mattress, she couldn't gain purchase, threatening to send them both tumbling off the bed. "Uh oh," she whispered.

From somewhere under the bed, one of the cats let out a *meow*.

Despite his sudden weariness—he had thought he was on the verge of passing out—John chuckled and managed to center himself on the bed with Ella Mae still atop him. He pulled her head down to his shoulder, grinning at hearing her giggles.

"Now, how is that?" His voice seemed to fade even as he tightened his hold on her body. "Are you comfortable?"

"I am."

"Good."

"You seem rather pleased with yourself, highwayman."

"Oh, I am," he admitted. He kissed the top of her head. "You should be, too."

Ella Mae gave a start, heartened at hearing his assessment. "When do you suppose we can do it again?" Despite how long it had been since he had pleasured her with his hand, tingles still darted through her, and awareness had her feeling more buzzy than the champagne had done the hour before.

She felt more than heard his chuckle beneath her body followed by an incoherent mumble and something about two more times before morning and every day after that.

"Two more times?" she repeated.

"*Meow.*"

"*Meow.*"

"Yes, according to the cats."

Ella Mae giggled and reached down to capture the edge of the counterpane. She pulled it over them before settling her head into the small of his shoulder.

She fell asleep with a grin on her face as Colonel and Sergeant joined them on the bed, their purrs sending the most pleasant vibrations through the bed.

"It is paawsitively heaven," she murmured.

ABOUT THE AUTHOR

A self-described nerd and lover of science, Linda Rae spent many years as a published technical writer specializing in 3D graphics workstations, software and 3D animation (her movie credits include SHREK and SHREK 2). Mythology, immortality, and ancient Greece have been lifelong interests.

A fan of action-adventure movies, she can frequently be found at the local cinema. Although she no longer has any tropical fish, she does follow the San Jose Sharks. She makes her home in Cody, Wyoming.

For more information:
www.lindaraesande.com
Sign up for Linda Rae's newsletter:
Regency Romance with a Twist
For articles on research and travels, read Linda's Rae
blog:
Regency Romance with a Twist

www.ingramcontent.com/pod-product-compliance
Lightning Source LLC
Chambersburg PA
CBHW030906200726
48289CB00003B/912